Merry Mischief and Cocoa Dreams: A Collection of Magical Christmas Tales

O. Q. Masterson

Published by Coledown Wells, 2023.

While every precaution has been taken in the preparation of this book, the publisher assumes no responsibility for errors or omissions, or for damages resulting from the use of the information contained herein.

MERRY MISCHIEF AND COCOA DREAMS: A COLLECTION OF MAGICAL CHRISTMAS TALES

First edition. December 3, 2023.

ISBN: 979-8223165682

Written by O. Q. Masterson.

Table of Contents

The Enchanted Snow Globe

Once upon a snowy Christmas Eve, in the cozy town of Evergreen Hollow, there lived a curious 8-year-old girl named Lily. Lily adored the holiday season, especially the magical stories her grandmother used to tell her. This year, Lily's grandmother had a special gift for her - a mysterious snow globe that had been passed down through generations.

As the clock struck midnight, Lily gazed into the snow globe, and to her astonishment, she was transported to a twinkling winter wonderland. The snowflakes sparkled like diamonds as she found herself in the heart of the North Pole. Standing before her was a jolly group of talking animals: a wise old owl, a playful reindeer, and a chatty polar bear.

The animals explained that Lily was chosen to help save Christmas, as the mischievous Jack Frost had stolen Santa's magical sleigh bells, causing a spell of gloom over the festive season. Determined to bring back the joy, Lily embarked on a magical journey with her newfound friends.

Their first stop was the Candy Cane Forest, where the trees were made of peppermint and gumdrops. The group encountered the Gingerbread Elves, who eagerly joined the quest. With their sugary wisdom, the elves guided Lily to the Frosty Mountains, where the mischievous Jack Frost was hiding.

Facing challenges and overcoming obstacles, Lily's courage shone brightly. Along the way, she discovered the true meaning of Christmas - kindness, generosity, and the joy of giving. The enchanted snow globe not only transported her to a magical realm but also transformed her heart.

In a climactic showdown with Jack Frost, Lily used the lessons she had learned to convince him to return the stolen sleigh bells. As the bells chimed once again, the gloom lifted, and the magic of Christmas was restored. Lily bid farewell to her newfound friends, returning to Evergreen Hollow just in time for Christmas morning.

When Lily awoke on Christmas Day, she found the snow globe by her bedside, a reminder of the extraordinary adventure she had experienced. As she opened her presents, she realized that the greatest gift was the love and warmth she could share with her family and friends.

And so, in the heart of Evergreen Hollow, as snowflakes danced outside her window, Lily understood that the magic of Christmas wasn't just in faraway lands but in the joy and love shared with those she cared about most. The enchanted snow globe became a cherished family heirloom, a symbol of the magical Christmas that changed Lily's life forever.

The Wondrous Workshop Woes

———

In the bustling village of Mistletoe Haven, nestled between frost-kissed hills and evergreen forests, there lived a spirited 9-year-old girl named Oliver. Christmas was his absolute favorite time of the year, and every December, he eagerly awaited the arrival of Santa Claus and his magical workshop.

One chilly evening, as the stars sparkled in the velvety sky, Oliver discovered a peculiar, old-fashioned key on his doorstep. Engraved with fantastical patterns, it seemed to hold a secret. Guided by his insatiable curiosity, Oliver followed a trail of shimmering dust that led him to a hidden entrance in the heart of the enchanted forest.

To his amazement, this entrance transported him to the Wondrous Workshop, a place beyond his wildest dreams. Greeted by animated toys and cheerful elves, Oliver marveled at the sight of a perplexed Santa Claus. The workshop was in disarray; the magical toy-making machinery had malfunctioned, and the joyous hum of Christmas had turned into a cacophony of clatters and whirrs.

With a determined twinkle in his eye, Oliver volunteered to help save Christmas. Guided by the Chief Elf, a quirky character with pointy ears and a penchant for inventing, Oliver embarked on a quest to fix the malfunctioning machinery. The adventure took them through the Candy Cogs and Nutcracker Nuts sectors, each filled with challenges that required a blend of creativity and problem-solving.

As Oliver and the Chief Elf delved deeper into the workshop's inner workings, they uncovered the mischievous Peculiar Pixies – tiny troublemakers who had sabotaged the machinery out of boredom. With clever negotiation and a sprinkle of kindness, Oliver convinced the pixies to join their cause. Together, they hatched a plan to restore order to the Wondrous Workshop.

Oliver, the Chief Elf, and the Peculiar Pixies worked tirelessly to fix the magical machinery. Along the way, they discovered the importance of teamwork, imagination, and the joy that comes from helping others.

As the first rays of Christmas morning painted the sky, the workshop hummed with a renewed energy. The repaired machinery whirred melodiously, and the toys sparkled with a magical glow. Santa Claus, with a twinkle in his eye, expressed his gratitude to Oliver and the newfound friends who had saved Christmas.

With a grateful heart, Oliver bid farewell to the Wondrous Workshop, returning to Mistletoe Haven just in time for a festive feast with his family. The enchanted key, now glowing with a warm radiance, became a cherished memento of the extraordinary adventure that unfolded in the heart of the magical forest.

And so, in Mistletoe Haven, as snowflakes gently fell, Oliver realized that the true magic of Christmas wasn't just in the presents under the tree but in the joy of bringing happiness to others. The Wondrous Workshop Woes became a cherished tale passed down through generations, reminding everyone that the spirit of Christmas lives in the kindness and imagination of those who believe in its magic.

The Mysterious Snowflake Symphony

In the charming town of Twinkleburg, where rooftops were dusted with snow and the aroma of freshly baked gingerbread wafted through the air, there lived a curious 8-year-old girl named Maya. Maya had always been fascinated by the magic of Christmas, but this year was different – an ethereal snowflake, unlike any other, appeared on her doorstep.

Captivated by its shimmering brilliance, Maya held the snowflake gently in her hands. Suddenly, a soft melody filled the air, and to her astonishment, the snowflake began to dance. It spun and twirled in harmony with the magical tune, creating a symphony of winter wonder.

Intrigued by this enchanting spectacle, Maya followed the dancing snowflake through the streets of Twinkleburg. The snowflake led her to the heart of the Enchanted Forest, a place where woodland creatures gathered to celebrate the spirit of Christmas. There, Maya met a whimsical ensemble of characters – a musical squirrel, a melodious rabbit, and a singing owl.

The woodland creatures explained that the Mysterious Snowflake Symphony was the key to unlocking the true magic of Christmas. However, an ancient spell had scattered the notes of the symphony across the enchanted land. Maya, with her heart full of wonder, volunteered to embark on a quest to retrieve the lost notes and restore the symphony.

Her journey took her through the Whispering Woods, where the trees whispered secrets of the past, and the Starlit Glade, where the gentle glow of fireflies guided her way. Along the way, Maya encountered challenges that tested her kindness, creativity, and resilience. She befriended a shy snowman with a magical hat and helped a group of mischievous snow sprites learn the joy of harmony.

As Maya collected each note of the Mysterious Snowflake Symphony, the melody grew more enchanting, weaving a magical tapestry in the winter air. The journey also taught Maya the importance of spreading joy and kindness, turning the quest into a heartwarming adventure of friendship and discovery.

Beneath the twinkling lights of the Grand Evergreen, Maya faced the ancient Snow Queen, the guardian of the final note. With courage and a heartfelt plea, Maya convinced the Snow Queen to release the last note, completing the Mysterious Snowflake Symphony.

As the symphony reached its crescendo, the entire Enchanted Forest lit up with a radiant glow. Snowflakes transformed into sparkling notes, swirling in a mesmerizing dance of light. The woodland creatures, along with Maya, joined hands, creating a magical moment that resonated with the true spirit of Christmas.

With the symphony restored, Maya found herself back in Twinkleburg, holding the now-glowing Mysterious Snowflake. As she shared her tale with the townsfolk, the once-sleepy town transformed into a festive celebration of lights, laughter, and joy. The Mysterious Snowflake Symphony had not only brought magic to Maya's life but had also infused Twinkleburg with the enchantment of Christmas.

And so, in the heart of Twinkleburg, as the snow fell gently, Maya realized that the true magic of Christmas wasn't just in the decorations or presents but in the melodies of kindness and the harmony of sharing joy with those you love. The Mysterious Snowflake Symphony became a cherished legend, inspiring generations to come with the magic of wonder and the spirit of Christmas.

The Whimsical Wonders of Wintertide

In the picturesque village of Frosthaven, where rooftops were adorned with twinkling lights and the aroma of cinnamon filled the air, lived a curious 7-year-old boy named Oliver. Oliver's eyes sparkled with wonder, especially during the festive season when the entire village buzzed with anticipation for the Grand Winter Festival.

One frosty morning, Oliver stumbled upon a peculiar invitation tucked between the pages of his favorite storybook. It was an invitation to the Secret Garden of Wintertide, a magical realm hidden behind a veil of sparkling icicles. Excitement bubbling in his chest, Oliver donned his warmest scarf and ventured into the unknown.

As he stepped through the shimmering portal, Oliver found himself in a world of whimsical wonders. The Secret Garden of Wintertide was a kaleidoscope of colors and enchantment, where talking snowmen exchanged jokes, and playful penguins waddled about with glee. In the center of the garden stood the Great Everfrost Tree, its branches adorned with mysterious ornaments that seemed to hum with magic.

Oliver soon discovered that the ornaments held the key to the festival's grand celebration. Each ornament possessed a unique ability, and to unlock the festivities, Oliver had to embark on a quest to gather them all. Guided by a mischievous snow sprite named Twinkle, he set off on a journey filled with riddles, puzzles, and heartwarming encounters.

His first stop was the Crystal Carousel, where the elegant horses whispered tales of winter magic. Oliver's task was to solve a puzzle to free the carousel's enchanting melody. With determination and a sprinkle of imagination, he succeeded, and the Crystal Carousel came to life, its music echoing through the Secret Garden.

Next, Oliver encountered the Giggling Glade, a realm filled with snow fairies who needed help gathering laughter to fill the laughter bulbs that adorned the Great Everfrost Tree. Oliver's contagious giggles and playful antics brought joy to the fairies, and soon, the laughter bulbs sparkled with warmth and mirth.

The journey continued through the Icicle Labyrinth, a maze of frozen wonders guarded by a friendly yet formidable snow dragon. Through clever negotiation and a game of frosty chess, Oliver won the dragon's trust, and the final ornament, shaped like a dragon's scale, joined the collection.

With the ornaments in hand, Oliver returned to the Great Everfrost Tree, where the Secret Garden erupted in a dazzling display of lights, music, and laughter. Villagers from Frosthaven were invited to the celebration, and as they entered the Secret Garden, their eyes widened with amazement at the whimsical wonders that unfolded before them.

The Grand Winter Festival became an annual tradition, and the Secret Garden of Wintertide opened its gates to spread joy and magic to all. Oliver, now a hero in the hearts of Frosthaven, continued to visit the Secret Garden each year, bringing new stories, laughter, and a touch of wonder to the festivities.

And so, in the heart of Frosthaven, as snowflakes danced in the glow of the festival lights, Oliver realized that the true magic of Christmas wasn't just in the presents or decorations but in the joy of creating unforgettable moments and sharing the wonders of the season with those you cherish. The Whimsical Wonders of Wintertide became a beloved tale, passed down through generations, reminding everyone that the magic of Christmas is a celebration of imagination, friendship, and the enchanting spirit that lives in the hearts of those who believe.

The Gleaming Guardian of Yuletide

———

In the quaint village of Frostington, where snowflakes painted the landscape in a delicate blanket of white and the aroma of hot cocoa filled the air, there lived a spirited 8-year-old girl named Emma. Emma had a heart as warm as the coziest fireplace, and her favorite time of the year was Christmas.

One frosty morning, as she strolled through the village square, Emma noticed a peculiar glow emanating from an old oak tree adorned with twinkling lights. As she approached, the glow intensified, revealing a tiny door nestled within the tree's gnarled bark. Intrigued, Emma opened the door and found herself in the cozy workshop of Jingle, the tiniest elf in all of Frostington.

Jingle, with a twinkle in his eye and a hat that jingled with every step, explained that Emma had been chosen as the Guardian of Yuletide – a magical responsibility passed down through generations. The task was to ensure that the Christmas Spirit, a radiant star held within a snow globe, remained aglow and vibrant. Without it, the village's festive cheer would dim.

Emma, with a heart full of excitement, accepted the responsibility and embarked on a journey to the Enchanted Forest, where the Snowflake Sprites guarded the gateway to the magical realm of Yuletide. There, she met Sparkle, the leader of the Sprites, and received the snow globe containing the precious Christmas Spirit.

However, as Emma made her way back to Frostington, a mischievous trio of Frostbats swooped down, stealing the snow globe and scattering its magical contents. Determined to save Christmas, Emma enlisted the help of Jingle and a talking robin named Merrywing. Together, they set off on a quest to retrieve the scattered Christmas Spirit.

Their first destination was the Tinsel Tundra, a glittering landscape where mischievous Glisten Gnomes guarded the first piece of the Christmas Spirit. Through a clever game of hide-and-seek, Emma outsmarted the gnomes, reclaiming the sparkling star that represented the joy of giving.

Next, they ventured to the Caroling Caverns, where a chorus of musical crystals held the second piece. Emma's kind and melodic voice, accompanied by Jingle's festive jingling and Merrywing's sweet chirps, resonated through the caverns, unlocking the musical magic within the crystal chorus.

Their journey led them to the Sugarplum Peaks, a land of candy canes and gumdrop mountains. There, the mischievous Frostbats had hidden the final piece of the Christmas Spirit. In a daring snowball fight that combined strategy and laughter, Emma and her companions reclaimed the last piece, restoring the snow globe to its full brilliance.

With the Christmas Spirit aglow, Emma returned to Frostington just in time for the village's annual Winter Festival. The restored snow globe radiated magic, bringing joy and warmth to the hearts of every villager. The once-sleepy village square transformed into a bustling celebration of lights, music, and laughter.

As Emma stood in the heart of the festivities, she realized that being the Guardian of Yuletide wasn't just about safeguarding the Christmas Spirit but also about sharing the magic of the season with others. The Gleaming Guardian of Yuletide, as she became known, continued to spread cheer and kindness throughout Frostington, creating a legacy that echoed through the years.

And so, in the heart of Frostington, as snowflakes gently fell, Emma understood that the true magic of Christmas wasn't just in the enchanting realms or magical responsibilities but in the warmth of friendship, the joy of giving, and the belief that every small act of kindness could light up the darkest winter night. The Gleaming Guardian of Yuletide became a cherished tale, passed down through generations, reminding everyone that the magic of Christmas lives in the hearts of those who keep the spirit of joy and love alive.

The Giggling Gumdrops of Jinglebell Junction

In the heart of Jinglebell Junction, a cozy town where snowflakes pirouetted in the wintry breeze and the air buzzed with the anticipation of Christmas cheer, lived a spirited 8-year-old girl named Penelope. Penelope, with her twinkling eyes and a heart full of mirth, was known for her infectious laughter that echoed through the snow-covered streets. Little did she know that this Christmas held a wondrous adventure that would sprinkle magic across Jinglebell Junction.

The heart of Jinglebell Junction was the Sugarplum Square, a bustling hub where shops adorned with peppermint stripes and ribbon-wrapped lampposts created a festive atmosphere. In the center of the square stood a colossal gumdrop tree, its branches adorned with glistening candies of every color. The tree, known as the Giggle Grove, was said to be the source of the town's laughter, and each year it produced a special batch of Giggling Gumdrops that spread joy to all.

As the snowflakes began to twirl in their wintry dance, Penelope felt a tingling in the air, a sign that the Giggle Grove was ready to produce its magical Giggling Gumdrops. Excitement bubbling within her, Penelope decided to embark on a quest to collect the Gumdrops and share their laughter with the town.

Guided by the glow of the peppermint lampposts, Penelope ventured into the Giggle Grove. The air sparkled with the enchantment of laughter as she approached the Gumdrop Guardian, a mischievous sprite with a hat made of candy wrappers.

"Hello, Penelope! The Giggle Grove is in need of your laughter. To collect the Giggling Gumdrops, you must embark on a laughter-filled journey," chirped the Gumdrop Guardian.

With a wink and a giggle, the Gumdrop Guardian handed Penelope a magical laughter jar, explaining that she needed to gather laughter from the various corners of Jinglebell Junction to fill the jar and awaken the Giggling Gumdrops.

Her first stop was the Tinsel Toy Emporium, a wonderland of playful gadgets and whimsical contraptions. Penelope, with her infectious laughter, engaged in a game of tickle tag with the toy soldiers and wind-up clowns. As their giggles filled the laughter jar, Penelope's heart swelled with joy.

Next, she visited the Cookie Cottage, where the aroma of freshly baked gingerbread wafted through the air. Penelope, with her love for sweets, joined Mrs. Gingerwhisk in a cookie decorating extravaganza. The frosting fights and sprinkles showered laughter like confetti, and Penelope merrily filled the laughter jar.

Her laughter-filled journey led her to the Merry Market, where townsfolk peddled festive goods and shared tales of holiday merriment. Penelope, with her friendly spirit, engaged in a laughter-filled storytelling circle. The tales of mischievous snow fairies and candy cane capers echoed through the market, and the laughter jar overflowed with the warmth of shared joy.

The final stop was the Jolly Jamboree, a lively gathering where carolers, jugglers, and magicians created a whirlwind of festive fun. Penelope, with her natural exuberance, joined the jamboree, dancing and laughing as though the world were a stage of merriment. The laughter jar, now brimming with the symphony of festive joy, radiated a magical glow.

With the laughter jar in hand, Penelope returned to the Giggle Grove. The Gumdrop Guardian, delighted by Penelope's laughter-filled adventure, sprinkled a dash of magic over the jar. The lid popped open, releasing a burst of sparkling laughter that echoed through the Giggle Grove.

From the branches of the Gumdrop Tree emerged the Giggling Gumdrops, small candies with tiny faces and infectious giggles. They hopped and skipped around Penelope, forming a circle of laughter that enveloped the entire Giggle Grove. The air, now filled with the joyous melodies of the Giggling Gumdrops, spread through Jinglebell Junction like a whimsical breeze.

The townsfolk, drawn by the laughter, gathered in Sugarplum Square. Penelope, surrounded by the Giggling Gumdrops, shared the tale of her laughter-filled journey. The Gumdrops, sensing the joy in the hearts of the townsfolk, multiplied, creating a cascade of laughter that wrapped the entire town in a cocoon of festive cheer.

As the laughter echoed through Jinglebell Junction, the snowflakes danced in joyful harmony, and the buildings shimmered with the magic of the season. The Giggle Grove, now illuminated with the laughter of the Giggling Gumdrops, became a symbol of the town's enduring merriment.

And so, in the heart of Jinglebell Junction, as snowflakes gently fell, Penelope understood that the true magic of Christmas wasn't just in the presents or decorations but in the shared laughter that connected the hearts of a community. "The Giggling Gumdrops of Jinglebell Junction" became a beloved tale, passed down through generations, reminding children that the spirit of Christmas is a celebration of joy, laughter, and the magic that happens when hearts come together in the spirit of merriment.

The Winterwish Wonders of Tinselville

———

In the wondrous town of Tinselville, where every building sparkled with festive lights and laughter echoed through the snow-covered streets, lived a spirited 8-year-old boy named Milo. Milo, with his twinkling brown eyes and a heart as warm as a cup of hot cocoa, was known for his boundless imagination and love for all things magical. Little did he know that this Christmas held a tale of enchantment that would unfold through the twinkling stars and shimmering ornaments of Tinselville.

One frosty evening, as the northern lights painted the sky with hues of emerald and lavender, Milo discovered an ancient book in the dusty corner of the town library. The book, titled "The Winterwish Chronicles," whispered tales of a magical comet that soared across the winter sky, granting wishes to those who believed in the wonders of the season. Intrigued by the stories, Milo set out on a quest to find the Winterwish Comet and make a wish that would fill Tinselville with joy.

Equipped with a tattered map and a heart full of wonder, Milo ventured into the Snowflake Forest, where each tree bore ornaments that glistened like jewels. The path, illuminated by the glow of enchanted fireflies, led him to the Sparkling Glade, a clearing where the Winterwish Comet was said to appear. As

Milo gazed at the starry sky, he whispered his heartfelt wish for Tinselville to experience the most magical Christmas ever.

To his amazement, the Winterwish Comet streaked across the sky in a dazzling display of colors. As it passed, a burst of magic showered the Sparkling Glade, and Milo felt a tingling sensation as if the very air was filled with the promise of wonder. The comet, leaving a trail of stardust, disappeared beyond the horizon.

Determined to unravel the magic woven by the Winterwish Comet, Milo followed the stardust trail to the Glistening Grove, a haven where luminescent snowflowers bloomed beneath the winter moonlight. Each snowflower, Milo discovered, held a unique magical ability granted by the comet. Guided by the shimmering glow of the flowers, he collected the Winterwish Petals, each radiating a different color and magic.

The first snowflower, with petals of silver, granted Milo the ability to understand the language of woodland creatures. The second, with petals of gold, bestowed upon him the power to bring festive decorations to life with a touch. The third, with petals of crimson, allowed him to create melodies that resonated with the joy of the season. The fourth, with petals of azure, gifted him the skill to craft enchanted snow sculptures that danced to the rhythm of the winter winds.

Milo, now equipped with the Winterwish Petals and their magical abilities, returned to Tinselville. The townsfolk, unaware of Milo's cosmic journey, were preparing for the annual Winter Wonderland Festival. The town square was adorned with twinkling lights, festive banners, and a towering Christmas tree that reached for the starry sky.

Eager to share the magic of the Winterwish Comet, Milo touched the first snowflake ornament, and to everyone's astonishment, it sprang to life, twinkling with newfound brilliance. The townsfolk, wide-eyed with wonder, witnessed the ornaments dancing in mid-air, creating a dazzling display that filled the square with gasps of delight.

Emboldened by the enchantment, Milo touched the second snowflake ornament. To the joy of the onlookers, wreaths and garlands came to life, twirling and weaving through the air like festive sprites. The town square transformed into a magical haven, with decorations alive with the spirit of the season.

As the townsfolk marveled at the animated decorations, Milo, with a mischievous smile, touched the third snowflake ornament. Melodies of joy and merriment filled the air as the enchanted ornaments harmonized in a magical symphony. The town square echoed with laughter and cheerful tunes, creating a festive atmosphere that warmed the hearts of all who gathered.

With the Winterwish Petals in hand, Milo approached the Christmas tree, adorned with a multitude of ornaments and shimmering lights. Touching the fourth snowflake ornament, Milo crafted a group of enchanted snow sculptures that twirled and danced around the tree. The sculptures, with each graceful movement, left trails of sparkles that added a touch of magic to the winter night.

The townsfolk, now caught in the midst of the Winterwish Wonders, joined Milo in a joyous celebration. Families danced beneath the animated decorations, children laughed as they chased after the enchanted snow sculptures, and the air buzzed with the magic of the season. Tinselville, bathed in the glow of the Winterwish Comet's magic, became a beacon of enchantment in the winter night.

As the festivities reached their peak, Milo stood in the center of the square, his heart aglow with the joy of sharing the Winterwish Wonders. Suddenly, the Winterwish Comet reappeared in the sky, casting a radiant light over Tinselville. Milo, feeling a surge of gratitude, whispered his thanks to the cosmic visitor, and the comet responded with a final burst of stardust that descended upon the town.

The stardust, carrying the magic of the Winterwish Comet, touched every corner of Tinselville. The townsfolk felt a warm embrace of cosmic enchantment, and their wishes for love, joy, and togetherness came alive in the glittering snowflakes that fell gently from the sky.

And so, in the heart of Tinselville, as snowflakes gently fell, Milo realized that the true magic of Christmas wasn't just in the decorations or presents but in the belief that wishes, no matter how big or small, could come true when hearts were filled with wonder and the spirit of the season.

The Gingerbread Grandeur

In the heart of Mistletoe Meadows, where snowflakes pirouetted in the wintry breeze and the air was sweet with the scent of festive delights, stood a charming bakery named "Sugarplum Sweets." This cozy establishment, with candy cane-striped awnings and a whimsical gingerbread façade, was owned by a spirited baker named Emma. Emma, with her twinkling hazel eyes and a heart as warm as the ovens in her bakery, was known for her magical confections that brought joy to the town. Little did she know that this Christmas held a tale of sugary enchantment that would unfold through the delectable delights of Sugarplum Sweets.

As the first snowflakes blanketed Mistletoe Meadows, Emma decided to create something extraordinary for the annual Winter Baking Contest. She locked herself in the bakery, surrounded by sacks of flour, jars of spices, and an array of enchanted ingredients that only she knew the secrets to. Inspired by a vintage recipe book left to her by her grandmother, Emma embarked on a confectionery adventure that would capture the essence of the holiday spirit.

Her creation? A magnificent Gingerbread Grandeur—a towering gingerbread castle adorned with spun sugar turrets, candy cane archways, and windows made of crystallized sugar. The aroma of cinnamon and ginger wafted through the air as the castle baked to perfection, its walls becoming a canvas for Emma's sugary artistry.

As Emma put the finishing touches on her masterpiece, a sprinkle of powdered sugar here, a dash of edible glitter there, the gingerbread castle came to life, emanating a magical glow that could rival the twinkling stars above Mistletoe Meadows. Little did Emma know, her enchanting creation had caught the attention of a mischievous Sugar Sprite named Sparkle, who resided in the enchanted Sugarplum Forest.

Drawn by the irresistible aroma of the Gingerbread Grandeur, Sparkle fluttered into Sugarplum Sweets with a twinkle in her eye. Emma, noticing the tiny sprite, greeted her with a warm smile. Sparkle, with her wings made of spun sugar and a dress woven from candy cane ribbons, explained that she was the Sugar Sprite Guardian of Sweet Wonders and had been drawn to the magical energy of the Gingerbread Grandeur.

With a mischievous wink, Sparkle sprinkled a pinch of Sugar Sprite Sparkle over the Gingerbread Grandeur, and to Emma's amazement, the castle came alive. Tiny gingerbread villagers bustled about, made of icing and sugar, and a warm, sugary glow enveloped the entire bakery. Emma's eyes widened with delight as she witnessed the sugary enchantment of her creation.

The news of the magical Gingerbread Grandeur spread like wildfire through Mistletoe Meadows. The townsfolk, drawn by the tales of the enchanted bakery, gathered outside Sugarplum Sweets. Emma, with a twinkle in her eye, opened the doors, inviting everyone to experience the sugary wonder within.

As the townsfolk entered the bakery, they were greeted by the sight of the Gingerbread Grandeur, now a bustling gingerbread village with houses made of candy canes, chocolate trees, and gumdrop gardens. Emma, guided by Sparkle's mischievous magic, invited the children to decorate their own gingerbread houses with sugary delights from the enchanted forest.

The bakery became a hive of activity, with laughter echoing through the air as families crafted their gingerbread masterpieces. The sugary villagers in the Gingerbread Grandeur joined the festivities, dancing and singing in joyous celebration. Emma, with her apron dusted in powdered sugar, watched with delight as the enchantment of the Gingerbread Grandeur brought the spirit of Christmas to life in Mistletoe Meadows.

As the sun dipped below the horizon, casting a warm glow over the town, Emma and Sparkle decided to take the celebration to the next level. With a wave of Sparkle's sugar wand, the Gingerbread Grandeur transformed into a magical stage, and the sugary villagers became performers in a whimsical sugar ballet.

The townsfolk gathered in awe as the gingerbread characters twirled and leaped, their movements accompanied by a sugary symphony. The air was filled with the sweet melodies of caramel notes and chocolate chords. Emma, with her baking spatula in hand, joined the performance, creating edible fireworks that burst in sugary sparks, illuminating the night with confectionery magic.

As the grand finale approached, Sparkle sprinkled one last pinch of Sugar Sprite Sparkle over the Gingerbread Grandeur. In an explosion of sweet magic, the enchanted village released a shower of edible snowflakes that drifted down from the gingerbread rooftops, creating a magical snowfall over Mistletoe Meadows.

The townsfolk, young and old, danced beneath the sugary snowfall, their hearts aglow with the enchantment of the Gingerbread Grandeur. Emma, with tears of joy in her eyes, realized that the true magic of Christmas wasn't just in the decorations or presents but in the shared moments of wonder and the sweet delights that brought hearts together.

As the clock struck midnight, signaling the end of the festive celebration, the Gingerbread Grandeur returned to its original form. The sugary villagers settled back into their gingerbread homes, and the enchanted glow faded away. Sparkle, bidding farewell to Emma, promised to return whenever the magic of the Gingerbread Grandeur was needed.

And so, in the heart of Mistletoe Meadows, as snowflakes gently fell, Emma understood that the true magic of Christmas wasn't just in the sugary wonders or enchanted delights but in the joy of sharing sweet moments with loved ones.

The Clockwork Toyshop: A Magical Mechanism of Wonders

———

In the heart of Frostvale, a quaint town where snowflakes danced on rooftops and the air was filled with the merry jingle of bells, nestled a peculiar shop known as "The Clockwork Toyshop." The shop, with its whimsical facade adorned with spinning gears and twinkling lights, was owned by a spirited toymaker named Oliver Winklebottom. Oliver, with his round spectacles perched on his nose and a heart as warm as molten cocoa, was known far and wide for crafting the most enchanting clockwork toys that brought joy to children's hearts. Little did he know that this Christmas held a tale of magical mechanisms that would unfold through the gears and springs of The Clockwork Toyshop.

As the first snowfall blanketed Frostvale, Oliver found a mysterious letter on his workshop doorstep. The letter, sealed with a golden wax crest of a clock and a twinkling star, bore an invitation to the Grand Mechanical Gala—an annual gathering of toymakers from across the enchanted realms. Intrigued by the prospect of sharing his clockwork wonders with fellow artisans, Oliver set out for the Gala, leaving his toyshop in the capable hands of his magical assistant, a tinkering sprite named Sparkplug.

The Grand Mechanical Gala, held in the heart of the Enchanted Workshop Woods, was a spectacle of whirling gears and tinkling melodies. Toymakers from realms far and wide showcased their fantastical creations—from flying toy dragons to clockwork carousels that spun under the starry sky. As Oliver wandered through the maze of marvels, he marveled at the ingenious creations that surrounded him.

At the center of the Gala stood a towering Clockwork Christmas Tree, adorned with twinkling lights and intricate clockwork ornaments. Oliver, inspired by the festive spirit, decided to create his masterpiece—a clockwork nutcracker that would dance to the tune of the Gala's magical melody. Guided by the whimsical wonders of the Enchanted Workshop Woods, Oliver worked tirelessly, crafting gears and springs with precision.

Unbeknownst to Oliver, Sparkplug, eager to assist his toymaker friend, decided to add a touch of extra magic to the nutcracker. Sparkplug, with a twinkle in his sprite eyes, sprinkled a dash of enchanted stardust over the completed creation. Little did he know that this impromptu addition would infuse the nutcracker with a magical spirit of its own.

As the clock struck midnight, signaling the end of the Gala, Oliver unveiled his clockwork nutcracker to the delight of the assembled toymakers. The nutcracker, with its polished brass exterior and silver gears, came to life in a burst of magical energy. It twirled and leaped with elegant precision, enchanting everyone with its mechanical dance.

Suddenly, the nutcracker paused mid-spin and turned toward Oliver with a nod of gratitude. To everyone's astonishment, the nutcracker began to speak in a soft, melodious voice.

"Thank you, Oliver Winklebottom, for bringing me to life. I am Nicholas, the Clockwork Guardian of Joy. As a token of my gratitude, I shall accompany you back to Frostvale and ensure that your toyshop is filled with wonders beyond imagination."

With that, Nicholas extended his hand, and Oliver, overcome with awe, accepted the nutcracker's offer of companionship. As they ventured back to Frostvale, Nicholas revealed his magical abilities. With a turn of his key, he could summon a snowstorm of enchanted snowflakes that danced in the wintry air. With a tap of his foot, he could create a trail of shimmering lights that adorned the streets like a celestial pathway.

Upon their return to The Clockwork Toyshop, Oliver and Nicholas found Sparkplug anxiously awaiting their arrival. Sparkplug, with a mischievous grin, explained that he had added a sprinkle of stardust to the nutcracker to enhance its magic. Oliver, though initially surprised, embraced the unexpected enchantment, realizing that Nicholas was more than just a clockwork creation—he was a guardian of joy.

As the news of Nicholas spread through Frostvale, children flocked to The Clockwork Toyshop to witness the magical marvel for themselves. Nicholas, with his graceful movements and whimsical magic, became the star attraction of the holiday season. The toyshop, now infused with the enchantment of the Clockwork Guardian, buzzed with excitement as children marveled at the wonders on display.

One chilly evening, as the townsfolk gathered in the town square, Nicholas took center stage for a special performance.

With a twirl of his key, he summoned a cascade of enchanted snowflakes that filled the air, creating a wintry spectacle. The children, wide-eyed with wonder, danced beneath the snowfall, their laughter echoing through Frostvale.

Nicholas, with a tap of his foot, illuminated the square with a celestial display of twinkling lights. The townsfolk, bathed in the magical glow, joined hands in a joyous dance. Oliver, watching from The Clockwork Toyshop, felt his heart swell with gratitude for the unexpected magic that had graced his humble toyshop.

As the clock tower chimed midnight, signaling the arrival of Christmas Eve, Nicholas gathered the children around The Clockwork Toyshop. With a twinkle in his eye, he produced a sack filled with miniature clockwork toys—tiny nutcrackers, dancing snowmen, and flying toy reindeer. Each child received a magical toy that would bring joy and wonder to their homes.

The town of Frostvale, now adorned with the magical marvels of The Clockwork Toyshop, became a haven of enchantment. Families gathered around their hearths, sharing tales of Nicholas, the Clockwork Guardian of Joy, and the wondrous creations that Oliver Winklebottom crafted with love and precision.

As Christmas morning dawned, Frostvale awoke to the sound of laughter and the twinkling of magical lights. The children, delighted by the clockwork toys bestowed upon them by Nicholas, reveled in the joy of the season. The Clockwork Toyshop, with its spinning gears and enchanted windows, stood as a testament to the magic that could be found in the most unexpected places.

And so, in the heart of Frostvale, as snowflakes gently fell, Oliver, Nicholas, and Sparkplug understood that the true magic of Christmas wasn't just in the decorations or presents but in the unexpected enchantments that filled the air when hearts were open to the wonders of the season.

The Starlight Sprinkles

In the quiet village of Frostford, nestled between snow-covered hills and evergreen forests, lived a spirited 8-year-old girl named Lily. Lily, with her twinkling blue eyes and a heart as warm as a cup of cocoa, was known for her love of winter adventures and the magical tales spun by the village storyteller, Old Man Winterglen. Little did she know that this Christmas held a story of its own—a tale woven with starlight and frosty enchantment that would unfold through the sparkling snowflakes of Frostford.

One frosty evening, as Lily wandered through the village square adorned with twinkling lights, she discovered a tiny door nestled between two frost-kissed trees. Intrigued, Lily opened the door, and to her amazement, she found herself in a glimmering, snow-covered meadow bathed in the soft glow of starlight. Before her stood a curious creature—a Frost Sprite named Twinkle.

Twinkle, with skin as translucent as ice and eyes that sparkled like winter stars, greeted Lily with a mischievous smile. "Greetings, Lily! I am Twinkle, the Frost Sprite of Frostford. I bring you tidings of a magical journey. Follow me, and you shall discover the secret of the Starlight Sprinkles."

Intrigued by the promise of magic, Lily followed Twinkle through the meadow, where the snow beneath her feet sparkled like a carpet of diamonds. The Frost Sprite led her to the

Starlight Glade, a magical clearing where ancient trees held the secret of the Starlight Sprinkles—the enchanted dust that brought dreams to life.

As they approached the Starlight Tree, Twinkle explained that each year, the tree bore star-shaped fruits filled with the mystical Starlight Sprinkles. These sprinkles, when scattered over the village on Christmas Eve, would bring forth the magic of winter and fulfill the deepest wishes of the villagers. However, this year, the Starlight Tree was bare, and the Starlight Sprinkles were nowhere to be found.

Determined to restore the magic, Lily and Twinkle embarked on a quest through Frostford. Their first stop was the Snowflake Silversmith, a wise old artisan who crafted delicate snowflakes from shimmering silver. Lily, with her artistic flair, joined the Silversmith in creating unique snowflakes that glistened like stars. The Silversmith, impressed by Lily's creativity, gifted her a special snowflake pendant that held a hint of frosty magic.

Their journey continued to the Enchanted Ice Skating Rink, where a group of Frost Fairies pirouetted on the ice, leaving trails of glittering frost in their wake. Lily, with her love for skating, joined the fairies in a graceful dance. As they twirled and spun, the Frost Fairies bestowed upon Lily a pair of enchanted ice skates that allowed her to glide effortlessly across the frost-kissed pond.

Their final destination was the Icicle Inn, a cozy tavern where villagers gathered to share tales and laughter. Lily, with Twinkle by her side, regaled the villagers with the story of the Starlight

Tree and their quest for the Starlight Sprinkles. The villagers, touched by the tale, offered their heartfelt wishes to the Starlight Tree and expressed gratitude for the winter magic it had bestowed upon Frostford.

As Lily and Twinkle returned to the Starlight Glade, they found the Starlight Tree still bare. Lily, with a determined look, placed the snowflake pendant around the tree's trunk and laced up her enchanted ice skates. With a deep breath, she twirled on the ice, scattering the glimmering snowflakes in a radiant dance. The Frost Sprite, inspired by Lily's actions, joined in the dance, creating a whirlwind of starlight and frost.

To their astonishment, the Starlight Tree responded with a gentle shiver. From its branches, star-shaped fruits began to appear, each filled with the coveted Starlight Sprinkles. Lily, with a twinkle in her eye, collected the magical dust in a sparkling pouch.

As Christmas Eve descended upon Frostford, Lily and Twinkle climbed to the highest hill overlooking the village. With a joyful heart, Lily scattered the Starlight Sprinkles over the rooftops, streets, and trees. The village sparkled in the magical dust, and as the clock struck midnight, a wondrous transformation occurred.

The snow-covered houses twinkled with starlight, and frosty patterns adorned the windows like intricate lace. Icicles hanging from the eaves chimed like crystal bells, and the air was filled with the laughter of delighted villagers. The Starlight Sprinkles had granted their wishes, bringing warmth, joy, and a sense of wonder to Frostford.

In the midst of the enchanted scene, Old Man Winterglen emerged from the village square. He, too, had a wish—to share one final tale with the children of Frostford beneath the starlit sky. The Starlight Sprinkles, attuned to the wishes of the villagers, created a magical storybook that floated into Old Man Winterglen's hands.

With a twinkle in his eye, Old Man Winterglen began to read a tale of frosty adventures and twinkling stars. The children gathered around, their hearts aglow with the magic of the Starlight Sprinkles. Lily, standing beside Twinkle, realized that the true magic of Christmas wasn't just in the decorations or presents but in the wishes that danced in the starlight and the enchanting tales that unfolded when hearts believed in the wonders of the season.

As the villagers of Frostford celebrated the magic of Christmas, Lily and Twinkle stood beneath the Starlight Tree, watching as the snowflakes continued to sparkle in the night. The Starlight Sprinkles had not only fulfilled the wishes of the villagers but had also woven a new tale—one of friendship, frosty enchantment, and the enduring magic that filled the air when starlight sprinkled its wondrous dust over the hearts of those who believed.

And so, in the heart of Frostford, as snowflakes gently fell, Lily and Twinkle understood that the true magic of Christmas wasn't just in the frosty landscapes or the glow of starlight but in the joy of sharing wishes, stories, and the whimsical tales that unfold when one believes in the power of the Starlight Sprinkles.

The Glistenberry Grotto

———

In the quaint village of Puddington, where the aroma of freshly baked puddings lingered in the air and cozy cottages were adorned with tinsel and lights, lived a curious 9-year-old girl named Rosie. Rosie, with her twinkling green eyes and a heart as sweet as sugarplums, was known for her love of all things pudding-related. Little did she know that this Christmas held a tale of magical wonders—a story woven with peculiar puddings and the magical mysteries of the Glistenberry Grotto.

One frosty morning, as the village prepared for the annual Pudding Parade, Rosie set out on her daily stroll through Puddington Park. The park, with its frosted trees and winding paths, held a secret known to only a few—the entrance to the Glistenberry Grotto. Legend had it that within the grotto, magical puddings of every flavor imaginable were created by the Pudding Pixies who resided there.

As Rosie reached the heart of the park, she noticed a peculiar sight—an opening beneath the roots of the Glistenberry Tree, the oldest and grandest tree in Puddington. Intrigued, Rosie crouched down and, with a sense of anticipation, crawled through the entrance. To her amazement, she found herself in the Glistenberry Grotto—a cavern filled with sparkling crystals and walls adorned with hanging pudding molds.

Rosie, wide-eyed with wonder, explored the grotto and soon encountered the Pudding Pixies—tiny, winged creatures with aprons made of spun sugar and pudding spoons for wands. The head Pixie, a spirited fellow named Berrywhisk, greeted Rosie with a twinkle in his eye.

"Ah, a visitor to our Glistenberry Grotto! Welcome, Rosie! We've been expecting you," exclaimed Berrywhisk, his wings shimmering with the magic of the grotto.

Rosie, filled with excitement, asked Berrywhisk about the magical puddings of the Grotto. The Pixies, delighted by Rosie's enthusiasm, explained that the Glistenberry Tree, with its radiant berries, produced the key ingredient for the most extraordinary puddings. However, this year, the berries were missing, and the magical puddings had not yet been created.

Determined to help, Rosie offered to embark on a quest to find the Glistenberry Berries and ensure that the Pudding Parade was filled with the most magical puddings ever tasted. Berrywhisk, touched by Rosie's willingness to help, provided her with a Pudding Passport—a magical map that would guide her through the festive realms of Puddington.

Rosie's quest began at the Frosty Frosting Falls, a cascade of sweet icing that sparkled like diamonds. The map led her to the Gingerbread Glade, where giant gingerbread men guarded the entrance to the Candy Cane Forest. With each step, Rosie discovered the sugary wonders of Puddington, from Peppermint Pathways to Marzipan Meadows.

As Rosie journeyed through the festive realms, she encountered peculiar characters, each with a sweet tooth and a love for puddings. The Licorice Leprechauns shared tales of rainbow-flavored puddings hidden at the end of the Candy Cane Rainbow, while the Toffee Turtles guided her through the Caramel Caverns in search of caramel-infused Glistenberries.

In the Cocoa Canyon, Rosie met the Cocoaberry Fairies, who, with a sprinkle of cocoa dust, enchanted the Glistenberries with the essence of chocolate. The Meringue Minstrels serenaded her in the Meringue Mountains, where whipped cream clouds floated in the sky. Each encounter brought Rosie one step closer to collecting the magical Glistenberries needed for the grandest puddings of the Pudding Parade.

As Rosie reached the final destination, the Sugarsnap Summit, she found herself standing before the Glistenberry Tree, a majestic sight with branches adorned with radiant berries of every hue. The tree, sensing Rosie's pure heart and love for puddings, bestowed upon her a golden spoon infused with the magic of the Glistenberries.

With the golden spoon in hand, Rosie harvested the Glistenberries, each one pulsating with the essence of the festive realms she had explored. The Sugarsnap Summit, resonating with the joy of the season, glowed in a kaleidoscope of colors as Rosie collected the last berry.

Filled with anticipation, Rosie returned to the Glistenberry Grotto, where the Pudding Pixies awaited her. Berrywhisk, with a joyful twirl of his wand, conducted a pudding-making ceremony. Rosie, guided by the magic of the Glistenberries and the Pudding Pixies' whimsical spells, created puddings of every flavor imaginable—sticky toffee figgy pudding, sparkling snowberry trifle, and frosted ginger-nut pudding.

As the puddings took shape, the Glistenberry Grotto resonated with the laughter and cheer of the Pudding Pixies. The puddings, infused with the magic of the festive realms, emitted a radiant glow that filled the grotto with a warm and inviting light.

With the puddings ready, Rosie and the Pudding Pixies set out for the Pudding Parade in the heart of Puddington. The villagers, awaiting the grand spectacle, gasped with amazement as Rosie and the Pixies emerged from the Glistenberry Grotto, carrying platters of the most extraordinary puddings ever created.

The Pudding Parade, now infused with the magic of the Glistenberry Grotto, became a joyous celebration of flavors and festive delights. Rosie, with a heart full of pride, led the parade through the streets of Puddington, where the aroma of the puddings wafted through the air, enchanting everyone who caught a whiff.

As the parade reached its climax, Rosie presented the grand finale—a towering Glistenberry Pudding, adorned with edible stars and sparkling sugar. The villagers, wide-eyed with wonder, gathered around the colossal creation as Rosie, with a flourish of her golden spoon, cut the first slice.

To everyone's delight, the Glistenberry Pudding revealed layers of festive flavors that danced on the taste buds—cranberry swirls, peppermint whispers, and a hint of enchanted cocoa. The magic of the Glistenberries, combined with Rosie's quest through the festive realms, had created a pudding unlike anything Puddington had ever seen.

The villagers, now filled with the warmth of the season and the joy of the Pudding Parade, joined in a festive feast beneath the twinkling lights of Puddington. Rosie, surrounded by friends and Pudding Pixies, realized that the true magic of Christmas wasn't just in the decorations or presents but in the unique flavors and sweet moments that brought hearts together.

As the night unfolded, Rosie gathered with the Pudding Pixies beneath the Glistenberry Tree. The tree, now adorned with a sprinkle of magical sparkles, resonated with the laughter and merriment of the villagers. Rosie, holding her golden spoon, thanked the Pudding Pixies for their whimsical guidance and the enchanting quest that had made the Pudding Parade a pudding peculiar spectacle.

And so, in the heart of Puddington, as snowflakes gently fell, Rosie and the Pudding Pixies understood that the true magic of Christmas wasn't just in the frosty landscapes or the glow of festive lights but in the unique flavors, delightful adventures, and the whimsical tales that unfolded when one believed in the power of pudding peculiar enchantment.

The Whispering Snowflakes

In the charming town of Frostington Falls, where the cobblestone streets glistened with a fresh layer of snow and the air was filled with the scent of peppermint and pine, lived a spirited 8-year-old girl named Mia. Mia, with her bright blue eyes and a heart as warm as a winter hearth, was known for her love of snowflakes and the enchanting tales spun by the town storyteller, Granny Frostwhisper. Little did she know that this Christmas held a story of its own—a tale woven with snowflakes and the magical mysteries of the Whispering Woods.

One frosty afternoon, as Mia strolled through Frostington Park, she noticed a peculiar phenomenon—the snowflakes seemed to twirl and dance in the air, whispering secrets that only she could hear. Intrigued, Mia followed the playful snowflakes as they led her to the edge of the park, where the towering pines gave way to a mysterious forest—the Whispering Woods.

Hesitant but curious, Mia stepped into the forest, the ground beneath her boots hushed by a carpet of snow. As she ventured deeper, the air became filled with a soft melody, the ethereal hum of the Whispering Woods. The snowflakes, now glowing with a gentle light, beckoned Mia to a clearing where a majestic snowflake tree stood, its branches adorned with shimmering crystals.

To Mia's astonishment, the snowflakes gathered around her, forming intricate patterns that seemed to tell a story. The tale spoke of a magical connection between the children of Frostington Falls and the enchanted snowflakes of the Whispering Woods. Every year, on the eve of Christmas, a chosen child would be granted the ability to hear the secrets of the snowflakes and embark on a quest to unlock the magic within the Whispering Woods.

Mia, chosen as this year's child, felt a surge of excitement as the snowflakes bestowed upon her a Frost Whisper Amulet—a delicate pendant that glowed with the essence of the Whispering Woods. Granny Frostwhisper's tales of ancient traditions and snowy wonders suddenly took on a new and magical meaning.

With the amulet around her neck, Mia set out on a quest guided by the whispers of the snowflakes. Her first stop was the Frosty Falls, a majestic waterfall frozen in mid-flow. The snowflakes guided Mia to a hidden cavern behind the falls, where a wise Ice Sage awaited. The sage, with a long white beard made of frost, explained that to unlock the magic of the Whispering Woods, Mia needed to gather three enchanted items—a Silver Frostleaf, a Crystal Frostdrop, and a Starlight Frostblossom.

The Frostleaf, the sage explained, could only be found in the heart of the Ice Crystal Caves, a labyrinthine system beneath the frozen peaks of Frosty Mountain. Determined and equipped with the Frost Whisper Amulet, Mia braved the icy tunnels, solving riddles and navigating shimmering caverns until she discovered the elusive Silver Frostleaf—a delicate silver leaf that shimmered with an otherworldly glow.

Her next destination was the Crystal Frostdrop, hidden within the Frostfire Grotto—an underground chamber where fire and frost coexisted in perfect harmony. Mia, guided by the whispers and the magical amulet, traversed the grotto's twists and turns until she found a crystalline pool. At its center floated the Crystal Frostdrop—a radiant droplet of frozen fire that captured the essence of the grotto's unique magic.

The final item, the Starlight Frostblossom, awaited Mia in the Celestial Glade—a clearing where the Whispering Woods met the starlit sky. Mia, entranced by the glow of the snowflakes, followed their ethereal trail until she reached the glade. There, beneath the celestial canopy, she discovered the Starlight Frostblossom—a delicate flower made of frost and stardust that pulsed with the magic of the heavens.

With all three enchanted items in hand, Mia returned to the snowflake tree in the heart of the Whispering Woods. The snowflakes, swirling around her in joy, guided Mia in arranging the items in a sacred pattern. As she did, the snowflake tree emanated a radiant glow, and Mia felt a surge of magic coursing through her veins.

The snowflakes, now forming a glittering pathway, led Mia to the heart of the Whispering Woods—a magical glade where ancient spirits of winter danced beneath the moonlit sky. Mia, with her amulet glowing brightly, joined the spectral dance, her every movement echoing the enchanting whispers of the snowflakes.

As Mia twirled and spun in the mystical glade, she felt a deep connection with the winter spirits and the magic that surrounded her. The Whispering Woods, resonating with the joyous dance, released a burst of magical energy that spread through Frostington like a winter breeze, touching the hearts of the townsfolk.

On Christmas Eve, as Mia returned to Frostington Falls, she found the town transformed. The snowflakes, now carrying the magic of the Whispering Woods, glistened with an ethereal light. The townsfolk, filled with a sense of wonder, gathered in the town square, where Mia shared the tale of her magical quest and the secrets of the Whispering Woods.

With a twinkle in her eye, Mia invited the townsfolk to join the Snowflake Soiree—a festive celebration where everyone could experience the magic of the snowflakes. As the night unfolded, Frostington Falls became a spectacle of twinkling lights, shimmering crystals, and the joyous laughter of the townsfolk.

In the town square, Mia stood with Granny Frostwhisper, who smiled with pride at Mia's journey and the magic she had brought to Frostington Falls. The snowflakes, now infused with the essence of the Whispering Woods, descended in a gentle flurry, forming intricate patterns that danced in the wintry air.

The children of Frostington Falls, inspired by Mia's tale, joined the Snowflake Soiree, twirling and dancing beneath the enchanting snowfall. The townsfolk, young and old, felt the magic of the Whispering Woods in their hearts—a connection that would linger long after the snowflakes had melted away.

As the clock struck midnight, signaling the arrival of Christmas Day, Mia and Granny Frostwhisper stood beneath the glittering lights of Frostington. Mia, with the Frost Whisper Amulet still aglow, felt a deep sense of gratitude for the magical journey that had unfolded.

And so, in the heart of Frostington Falls, as snowflakes gently fell, Mia and the townsfolk understood that the true magic of Christmas wasn't just in the decorations or presents but in the whimsical wonders, frosty friendships, and the enchanting tales that unfolded when one believed in the power of the Whispering Snowflakes.

The Enchanted Tinsel: A Sprinkle of Stardust Magic

In the whimsical village of Starhaven, nestled between rolling hills and beneath a sky sprinkled with constellations, lived a spirited 8-year-old girl named Ella. Ella, with her twinkling eyes and a heart as bright as a comet, was known for her love of all things celestial and the magical tales spun by the village astronomer, Professor Stardust.

One evening, as the first snowflakes began to fall and the village prepared for the annual Starlight Celebration, Ella wandered through Starhaven Park. The park, adorned with twinkling lights and celestial decorations, held a secret known to only a few—the entrance to the Stardust Gateway. Legend had it that beyond the gateway lay the Stardust Galaxy, a realm of stardust magic where wishes were granted through the power of enchanted tinsel.

Intrigued by the legend, Ella followed the path of sparkling lights until she reached the Stardust Gateway. To her amazement, the gateway opened, revealing a celestial pathway that led to a realm bathed in the glow of stardust. Ella, with a heart full of wonder, stepped into the Stardust Galaxy.

As she traversed through the galaxy, Ella encountered Stardust Sprites—tiny, luminous beings with wings that glowed like shooting stars. The head Sprite, a radiant figure named Lumina, greeted Ella with a sparkle in her eyes.

"Welcome, Ella! We've been expecting you," Lumina exclaimed. "The Stardust Galaxy responds to those who carry the light of the stars in their hearts. You, dear child, are destined to bring the magic of enchanted tinsel to Starhaven."

Lumina explained that each year, on the eve of the Starlight Celebration, a chosen child from Starhaven would visit the Stardust Galaxy to collect the Enchanted Tinsel. This magical tinsel, when sprinkled over the village decorations, would infuse the Starlight Celebration with an extraordinary brilliance.

Determined to embrace her celestial destiny, Ella was gifted a Celestial Scepter—a wand adorned with a radiant star that resonated with the magic of the Stardust Galaxy. With Lumina as her guide, Ella set out on a quest to collect the Enchanted Tinsel from three celestial realms—the Sparkling Nebula, the Comet's Trail, and the Moonlit Mirage.

Her first stop was the Sparkling Nebula, a breathtaking expanse of swirling colors and ethereal lights. Lumina led Ella to the heart of the nebula, where Stardust Sprites danced among the cosmic clouds. Ella, with her Celestial Scepter in hand, joined the Sprites in a celestial dance, creating a luminous trail of stardust that would become the Sparkling Tinsel.

Next, they ventured to the Comet's Trail, where shimmering comets streaked across the night sky. Ella, guided by Lumina's wisdom, hopped from comet to comet, collecting stardust and celestial gems that would transform into the Comet's Trail Tinsel—a sparkling creation that captured the magic of cosmic journeys.

Their final destination was the Moonlit Mirage, a tranquil realm where the moon cast a gentle glow over a field of silver flowers. Ella, with Lumina by her side, gathered moonbeams and infused them with stardust to create the Moonlit Tinsel—a silver-hued enchantment that reflected the serenity of the moonlit night.

As Ella returned to Starhaven, her Celestial Scepter aglow with the magic of the Stardust Galaxy, the villagers gathered in anticipation of the Starlight Celebration. Ella, with Lumina and the Stardust Sprites by her side, sprinkled the Enchanted Tinsel over the village decorations.

To everyone's delight, the tinsel emitted a radiant glow, and the entire village sparkled like a celestial wonderland. The Starlight Celebration, now infused with the magic of the Stardust Galaxy, became a spectacular event that captivated the hearts of the villagers.

As the night unfolded, Ella and Lumina stood at the heart of Starhaven, watching as the enchanted tinsel cast a celestial aura over the village. The Stardust Sprites, with their wings aglow, danced in the wintry air, leaving trails of stardust that shimmered like cosmic ribbons.

In the midst of the celebration, Professor Stardust emerged from his observatory, his eyes wide with amazement. He approached Ella, his celestial apprentice, and congratulated her on bringing the magic of the Stardust Galaxy to Starhaven.

With a twinkle in his eye, Professor Stardust invited the villagers to join in a cosmic storytelling session. Ella, now a heroine of the Stardust Galaxy, shared tales of her celestial quest and the magical realms she had explored. The villagers, enchanted by the stories and the celestial wonders above, reveled in the joy of the Starlight Celebration.

As midnight approached, signaling the arrival of Christmas Day, Ella gathered with Lumina and the Stardust Sprites beneath the Cosmic Arch—the central decoration of the Starlight Celebration. With a wave of her Celestial Scepter, Ella summoned a cascade of stardust that formed a celestial pathway in the sky.

The Stardust Sprites, now forming a celestial choir, sang a melody that echoed through the village. Ella, with Lumina by her side, led the villagers beneath the Cosmic Arch in a final dance, their hearts aglow with the magic of the Stardust Galaxy.

And so, in the heart of Starhaven, as snowflakes gently fell, Ella and the villagers understood that the true magic of Christmas wasn't just in the decorations or presents but in the celestial wonders, stardust magic, and the enchanting tales that unfolded when one embraced the cosmic brilliance of the season.

The Jinglebell Jamboree

In the delightful town of Giggleville, where laughter echoed through the cobblestone streets and every day felt like a merry celebration, lived a spirited 8-year-old girl named Binny. Binny, with her twinkling brown eyes and a heart as bubbly as a cup of hot cocoa, was known for her infectious laughter and the playful tales spun by the town's Chief Jester, Jinglewiggle. Little did she know that this Christmas held a story of its own—a tale woven with whimsical giggles and the mischievous wonders of the Giggly Grotto.

One frosty morning, as the town prepared for the annual Giggly Gala, Binny skipped through Giggleville Park, her laughter trailing behind like a string of jinglebells. To her surprise, the laughter seemed to guide her to a hidden entrance beneath the Giggly Grove—a passage that led to the heart of the Giggly Grotto.

Intrigued and giggling all the way, Binny descended into the Grotto—a cavern filled with sparkling crystals and walls adorned with hanging stockings that jingled with every gust of laughter that echoed within. Before her stood a peculiar creature—a Gigglesprite named Wobblewhisk.

Wobblewhisk, with a round belly that jiggled like a bowl of jelly and eyes that twinkled with mischief, greeted Binny with a hearty chuckle. "Ahoy there, Binny! I'm Wobblewhisk, the

Gigglesprite of Giggleville. We've been expecting you for the Jinglebell Jamboree. Follow me, and let the giggles guide you!"

Intrigued by the promise of a jamboree, Binny followed Wobblewhisk through the Giggly Grotto, where the laughter seemed to bounce off the walls like joyful echoes. The Gigglesprite led her to the Jinglebell Junction, a whimsical clearing where mischievous giggles floated through the air like confetti.

Wobblewhisk explained that every year, on the eve of Christmas, the Jinglebell Jamboree unfolded in the heart of the Giggly Grotto. This magical celebration was fueled by the laughter and giggles of the town's children, which were collected in the Jinglebell Jars—the mystical containers that held the essence of joy and merriment.

To Binny's amazement, the Jinglebell Jars were scattered across the Giggly Grotto, each guarded by a Giggleguard—a mischievous guardian who tested the giggling skills of anyone attempting to collect the laughter. Wobblewhisk, confident in Binny's laughter prowess, handed her a Giggleguide—a map that revealed the locations of the Jinglebell Jars and the challenges that awaited.

Binny, with her gigglesome spirit in full swing, set out on the Jinglebell Jamboree adventure. Her first stop was the Tinseltangle, a maze of sparkling tinsel that seemed to shift and shimmer with every step. Giggleguards, camouflaged in the tinsel, challenged Binny to a game of Gigglehide-and-seek. Binny's laughter, infectious and full of glee, echoed through the

Tinseltangle, revealing the hiding Giggleguards who surrendered their Jinglebell Jars with a mischievous grin.

Next, Binny ventured to the Jollyjump Junction, where trampolines made of candy canes propelled her into the air with each leap. Giggleguards bounced alongside Binny, engaging her in a game of Giggleleap. As Binny giggled and bounced, the Giggleguards surrendered their Jinglebell Jars, delighted by the contagious merriment.

Her final challenge awaited in the SnickerSnare Swamp, a bog filled with marshmallow quicksand and candy cane vines. Giggleguards, disguised as marshmallow creatures, challenged Binny to a game of Gigglebalance. Binny, with her nimble feet and infectious laughter, danced across the marshmallow terrain, causing the Giggleguards to burst into fits of giggles. In appreciation, they handed over their Jinglebell Jars.

With all the Jinglebell Jars in hand, Binny returned to Jinglebell Junction, where Wobblewhisk awaited. The Gigglesprite, with a twinkle in his eye, led Binny to the center of the clearing—a Giggleglade adorned with sparkling lights and jingling decorations.

As the clock struck midnight, the Jinglebell Jamboree commenced. Binny, surrounded by Giggleguards, Gigglesprites, and the laughter-filled atmosphere of the Giggly Grotto, began to sprinkle the collected giggles into the Giggleglade. The Jinglebell Jars, now empty, echoed with the laughter of Giggleville's children, creating a symphony of joy that filled the air.

To Binny's amazement, the laughter began to transform into whimsical creatures—Gigglefairies, Jinglegnomes, and Chucklechimeras. These creatures, fueled by the pure laughter of the town's children, danced and twirled in the Giggleglade, creating a spectacle of giggles and merriment.

As the Jinglebell Jamboree unfolded, the laughter-filled creatures spread across Giggleville, visiting every home and spreading infectious joy. The town, now aglow with the magic of the Giggly Grotto, became a whimsical wonderland where laughter echoed in every corner.

In the midst of the Jinglebell Jamboree, Chief Jester Jinglewiggle emerged from the town square, his hat adorned with jingling bells. He joined Binny in the Giggleglade, his laughter harmonizing with the laughter of the magical creatures. Together, they led the townsfolk in a dance of giggles, creating a jubilant celebration that would be remembered for years to come.

As the first rays of Christmas Day peeked over the horizon, Binny and the townsfolk gathered in the heart of Giggleville. The laughter-filled creatures, now returning to the Giggly Grotto, left behind a trail of sparkles and jingles. Binny, holding her Giggleguide as a cherished souvenir, realized that the true magic of Christmas wasn't just in the decorations or presents but in the giggles that echoed through the town, creating a tapestry of joy and merriment.

And so, in the heart of Giggleville, as snowflakes gently fell, Binny and the townsfolk understood that the true magic of

Christmas wasn't just in the festivities or decorations but in the giggles that echoed through the town, creating a tapestry of joy and merriment.

Milton Keynes UK
Ingram Content Group UK Ltd.
UKHW020748111223
434160UK00016B/882